Published by LSL BOOKLETS
LIQUOR STORE LIT ™ is a Jim Lopez Creation
liquorstorelit.com
Los Angles

Cover Design by Jim Lopez © 2011

ISBN 13 978-0692278970
ISBN 10 0692278974

For other works by Jim Lopez see
jimlopez.org
antiquechildren.com

Part 1 of 2

VINNIE BANG BANG &

THE CHEMICAL PUNK MONKEY

GENERATION PB82

JIM LOPEZ

"The Last Dregs of Poverty"
Series

One man cannot mobilize the spontaneous capacity of the masses.

A vigorous fuck with a stiff upper lip in a sprawling mess, bubbling at a critical temperature in a pot of jig-a-boo soup, was the day Old One Eye went to the Musky Optometrist and saw the world for the first time with two eyes. Mutants understood that the Nightmare of Recrimination was the mere unfolding of a story about a mutant who dreamt of uniting with a life partner.

The days of naught, of nil, the center of nothing, without quantity, without quality, deficient in value, a world devoid of genius characterizing the disfigurement of form, and the lack of imagination and inspiration infected Vinnie Bang Bang and the Chemical Punk Monkey's Generation Pb82. The signifying of the mythical magnitude of the Zenithal, the Zeitgeist of Zero, the supreme deity, Mr. Zig-Zag, brother to Zeus, in The Years of Zilch, where friends had the decency to be alienated, resembling broken eggs devoid of any yolk: signifiers that the Wild Life was the ever so *rare* Exotic Life.

To live in the world, which adorned its lapels with the emblematic avatar "SCR" (Social Construction of Reality), one learned to reduplicate behavior, things, that which was best in a person in order to succeed. Getting a cock in the ass was nothing more than a cotton swab wound that helped a mutant see the world through the eyes of the projectionist, who spent his evenings pulling his mudskipping pud-stump in the back of the theater; that is to say, God had become a cynical masturbator.

Vinnie Bang Bang and the Chemical Punk Monkey refused to reduplicate behaviors that the broken down, defunct SCR programmed for success; however, they did develop a daily routine of dumpster diving, and it was this unattractive form of habitual treasure seeking that would paradoxically lead to an invite to the stankiest love fest in town. Luck had smiled upon these two garbage goblins, mutants of Generation Pb82. Vinnie Bang Bang and Chemical Punk Monkey had found a ham radio, a moldy eggplant and a fresh head of lettuce: three valuable objects worthy of exchange for admittance to the blow and go show.

There was nothing like the smell of a burning barrel at the end of the street. The only scent considered sweeter was the odor of unwashed vagina. And few mutants had the pleasure of having it run through their nostrils and infecting their senses. Most of the brick and mortar that lined buildings had been removed long ago. All that remained was the rust of steel and the acrid smell of lead in the air. Good for warming the hands but bad for the balls. Men were dribbling semen the way old women dripped the clap down their rumpled panty hose. No young mutant could find his way through this mess, especially when he knew it was his granny who laid spread eagle for the neighborhood dork to cop a poke.

"Martin Luther King Jr. might have been right for his time but he is wrong for our time!" resounded from a megaphone held by a small, toothless man, wearing a doctors smock and fishnet stockings, with a hooked nose screwed to his face, tattoos defining his skin pigmentation, as he gyrated like James Brown screaming, "Hot Pants!"

Chemical Punk Monkey's grandmother had read him everything that Martin Luther King Jr. had written, at least everything that survived the savage burn of the early 21st Century. Chemical Punk Monkey's grand-mother read him the revolutionary prose of Marcuse, Cornel West, Che, Castro, Marcos, esoteric philosophies, hermetic Gnosticism, cynical antics of shit-tossing primates, and the usual libidinous buggaries of John Wilmot, the 2nd Earl of Rochester. And who needed it? None of it amounted to a damn thing: just words and the illusions of a human utopia: no real statistical plans capable of being implemented to overthrow corruption and avarice. Chemical Punk Monkey was losing hope as his memories grew sharper, and his need for justice waned.

In the 19th century a town developer needed whores to maintain a firm grasp upon his labor force, so he bought some, women that is. He built his whores a house, hung a sign and opened for business. The budding towns-men were hired laborers, consisting mostly of Northern Europeans and fresh-off-the-boat Chinks, who kept to themselves. These were men who turned out their pockets for the last time in their native lands; men who possibly sought a better life or who simply moved from one coin to the next spending it on the only woman they ever had the privilege of meeting: a whore. These men were born from whores and they tallied up to be an excellent resource for labor: a valuable and inexpensive expression of man power with nothing to lose and less to hope for.

The town developer needed to keep these men working, and he sure as hell needed to make damn sure that they never saved their pittance and achieved a little bit of the better life. So the town developer housed his men moderately, cutting as much cost as possible without diminishing his labor force, opened up a whore house and bar, which facilitated steady employment for the growing female population

and the hops farmers. Then he successful-
ly manipulated his labor force, that is, the
flesh and blood of the town builders, who
spent their money in the town they had a
hand in erecting. The developer exploited
his labor force while giving them a com-
munity where a man can pursue and ob-
tain two of the most cherished pursuits in
life: the feeling up of wenches and the bliss
of drink; the third being wisdom but every
man must pursue her according his own
constitution and love for her. And if all a
man ever wants is to have a few drinks, lay
with a woman, and all the warmth her wet
pussy has to offer for a few bucks, leaving
the old country, which didn't want him any
way, and grinding out his labor for a little
more than a few bucks to buy a bottle and
some non-judgmental pussy, pounding out
a living wasn't that bad of a life. He could

get drunk, fucked, and forget about the meaningless labor that morning would demand of him.

Hollywood no longer had a need for many whores. The movie industry was dead. Besides, the town developers sold the City to a Jap, a kike, and a Christian prick, who dumped the labor force and sailed away with the winter canaries.

Jumbo's Clown Room was one of the last places a mutant could see a woman: a woman who danced on stage, climbed a pole and stuck to mirrors, as she removed all her ragged clothes and revealed what granny and the clap never dared to show but was happy to throw in the gutter. Old granny had become a cum guzzling gutter slut with from-under-cheese coagulating between her labia. The old broken down bitch lied in back alleys, alongside garbage cans, discarded rat bones and plaques of roaches. Most of the mutant boys, as well as some female mutants, had gone to see her, and they did so with sincere gratitude. Granny gum pucker was the only love around and no mutant ever raised a complaint; however, the occasional few settled for one of her shit biscuits buttered with rat lard and sprinkled with pigeon shit. When gutter tramp granny is the only love in town it's not unusual for a mutant to go scratching his crotch, scrounging for old granny's dirty cookie through alleyways day or night.

People loathed one another, feigning good times at busted down leaky bars where a tomato could get a mutant a shot of rancid testicle yeast. This was Generation Pb82. The general population had begun mutating about thirty years ago. In the beginning of the mutation era people were first stricken with malignant tumors and rudely dropped dead while waiting in line to use the toilet at baseball games. Cancer had wiped out most of the general public. Of course, those with excellent health care were able to avoid most of the disgraceful disfigurements. Those who paid out the nose for lousy health care died and those with no health care mutated into "obscene" creatures.

Chemical Punk Monkey began his mutation process at the age of one-in-a-half. Little by little his face grew hair, his eyesight sharpened, his hearing became more acute, his appetite for chemically modified bananas and grapefruit affected the development of his cock and balls, which were extraordinarily small and/or ridiculously huge, depending on the angle of one's view: a completely inconsistent phenomenon of the genital growth pattern.

Vinnie Bang Bang's mutation started in his fourth year of life. He was standing blind-folded under a piñata, waving a brown stick in one hand and a red hot chili pepper in the other, when he was struck with the acute and eerie sensation of knowing right where to bust the flying piñata's ass wide open. When he swung and struck, an artificial smell of tittie juice came showering down upon him. His pubic hair grew soft like a lamb's ear and his cock developed multiple limbs not unlike the mysterious Banyon Tree. His fingers began to curl. His chest barreled, and his cranium bulged tight against his orange beanie cap. When the piñata finished pissing it's after-birth on him, Vinnie Bang

Bang was left dripping wet, looking like an old time *vatoreno* walking with a limp and a cane. Vinnie Bang Bang was only four-years-old, but he had mutated into a third generation *vato* from East Los Angeles. Many referred to him as Vince the Pinch but those who enjoyed his company most knew him as Vinnie Bang Bang.

Martin Luther King Jr. was right for his times but he was definitely not right for the Chemical Punk Monkey and Vinnie Bang Bang's time. In fact, King Jr. was hell-a wrong.

The smell of pussy had become so scarce no one understood the essence of pursuit or the pleasure of the journey any longer. Men had long ago forgotten the advantage of holding council in the presence of women. There were no longer any sound solutions. All that remained was the carcasses of decaying genitals. One truth remained certain: the people's purchasing power hadn't amounted to shit. And the scent of Josephine's unwashed salty cunt had grown faint while waiting for Napoleon to finish beating his meat, as he contented himself in a never ending quest for self-engagement.

Chemical Punk Monkey and Vinnie Bang Bang had never known the smell of unwashed vagina, let alone clean vagina, if there was such a vagina. They had heard stories, tales told outside of school, but the only pussy these two mutants had ever smelled was the shed linings of a uterus soaked into a bloody tampon, which was stuck to the bottom of a garbage bin. Pussy had dried up so tight that the Plutocracy went on a purchasing frenzy buying up 95% of the love lips out on the streets. A mutant could not find poontang anywhere. But Jumbo's Clown Room had a voltage line straight to Washington's Red Light District.

Chemical Punk Monkey had been wearing the same pair of dumpster divers (Chuck Taylors) for the last eight years. His feet had begun to mutate and now what was once his left foot was now his right and vise-a-versa. He and Vinnie Bang Bang had found a fairly fresh head of lettuce, a slowly rotting eggplant and a busted ham radio, which still picked up static in the airwaves, in a dumpster in an alley near Los Feliz Village, and made their way to Jumbo's Clown Room, where they traded their treasure for a night at the Cunthole Carnival.

A rumor had been circulating that a UCLA Dance Major coupled with a Lot

Lizard were performing a strip tease that left the stink of unwashed pussy on a mutant's upper lip for three days. What did these two strippers have in common? They were both lactating and neither one of them had ever been pregnant. Needless to say, for Vinnie Bang Bang and the Chemical Punk Monkey, this was like hitting the Florida Lottery when there was still an economy worth more than a pound of shit to heat the house. A ham radio, moldy eggplant and fairly fresh head of lettuce would not only get them through the front door, they'd be greeted with a shot of titty milk tonight, after which new doors would be opened for the two mutants.

The stink of Social Construction of Reality was like having one's head rammed up a rhino's ass, while it was being speared by niggers in Africa and gangbanged by red necks from Langley. Filthy pussy on one's upper lip bought some time from suicide's inevitability.

Vinnie Bang Bang and Chemical Punk Monkey wanted out of the banality of fabricated hysteria and rancid poon was their only way out. But it wasn't cheap. Normally, one had to act like an asshole to gain admittance; whereas, Lady Luck graced Chemical Punk Monkey and Vinnie Bang Bang when they went rummaging through a dumpster that morning.

Vinnie Bang Bang was, of course, fingering some hermaphroditic mutant of unknown origin, as Chemical Punk Monkey was scavenging for a rotten banana or a dirty prune to eat for breakfast, while trying to forget the image of his younger brother huffing granny's girdle the night before. Chemical Punk Monkey was a true believer; dreaming of the good life, hoping to find something that at the very least *felt* more meaningful. And now he and Vinnie Bang Bang just might have found that which they never had: an escape from the feeble futility of the world running through itself like a vacuum at an abortion clinic.

Chemical Punk Monkey took a shot of some sort of grain alcohol distilled in decomposing Styrofoam and wandered into Jumbo's Clown Room. Vinnie Bang Bang slurped from a puddle left behind from a Mexican ditch party and be-bopped through the door with little help from his cane; however, he was immediately accosted by a large-titted transvestite wearing a tank-top with "These Are Mommy's" spray painted across her silicon boltons. Her schlong was curved like Aladdin's sword and she was attempting to slice Vinnie Bang Bang in half. Vinnie Bang Bang ducked and weaved till he landed one on the bitch, dropping her back into the hole under the bar, from which she crawled out of.

Jumbo's Clown Room housed all types of mutant women, from gentle ladies to homicidal fag hags.

Chemical Punk Monkey had vaginal semen sprayed into his eyes and a bag of freshly shaved public hairs blown into his monkey face. The exact sexual identity of the Squirter was unknown. Chemical Punk Monkey thought he had been blinded while waging personal jihad, and he had been, momentarily blinded that is. The moment he found that ham radio, moldy eggplant and fairly fresh head of lettuce he was struck with the clarity he had always been looking for, but now he had a minge hair lodged under his eyelid, scratching his cornea.

Vinnie Bang Bang and the Chemical Punk Monkey discovered what everyone who had ever walked into Jumbo's Clown Room had discovered: one was obligated to get finger-fucked in the first three minutes of arrival, sometimes sooner. Anti-monopolistic sentiment ran rampant. Every mutant was an independent; however, he was wholly dependent upon the monopoly to plug a finger up someone's ass. Give a little, get a little, get pounded, get blasted, get pounded again, do a little blasting of your own, balls stretched to the floor, pussy plapulating to the song of Pandora's Box...

The photo interpretation began to melt when the first load of drugs circulated through the room: chemically potent rainbow pills masked with the sugary taste of an elixir sure to distort perception. Long Term Capital Management unwound from the stripper pole, sticky with ass juice. Over the Counter Derivatives filled napkin boxes placed on tables near the lap dance booth, hidden like landmines in a battle field. The only mechanical regulator was an old black man with a large gray beard and six fingers, three on each hand. He played Sam Cooke's "A Change Is Gonna Come" on a busted-up, out-of-tune piano: only no change ever came.

The stage show started with a Tease, romping her rump to the meat of the music, which was followed by three acts of male mutants molesting the audience. A toad who mutated into the immortal Henry Kissinger, with his fat ass slobbering on the edge of the stage, spitting out sweaty wads of dollar bills from his spider button, was the first to get gang rapped. What was most vulgar was that he knew better than to believe that dollars had value and then try to pass them onto the punch drunk mutant dancer at Jumbo's Clown Room. A can of Cambell's Chicken Noodle Soup could have gotten the cock sucking Kissinger what he was looking for; that is, a pint of jizz blasted in his mug. Instead, he was corn-holed, from both ends, and tossed out into the alley. At first, he thought he'd slipped face first into the creamy Milky Way. When he discovered a chocolate bar had been shoved up his shithole he sucked it out himself and ate it. This would be all he would eat for a week, until he behaved like a big enough asshole so that Jumbo's Clown Room felt obliged to invite him back in, only to have things done to him that were rumored too disgraceful to describe, but kept him fed for the rest of his immortal life, never to experience death by misadventure.

In the world of Generation Pb82 Dostoevsky would never have been favored with exile. He would have been whipped senselessly, then stripped naked, tied to the back of a garbage truck and drug through the streets of every ghetto in the industrial-chemical world. By the time the last ghetto got a look at him all that would remain of him would be his shredded hands, minus a few fingers, hanging from the bumper.

Vinnie Bang Bang and the Chemical Punk Monkey thought they'd never find true, romantic love. You know, the kind of love the Rosicrucians described as the completion of man and woman coming together. Instead, they'd finger-bang their way through garbage cans the rest of their useless lives until the Pie in the Sky favored them with Lady Luck's winking brown eye.

To Be Continued...

Vinnie Bang Bang & the Chemical Punk Monkey meet Boom Boom Ophelia & Bunny Jungle Butt. Do they fall in love and escape to the island of Malta or does everything fall apart?

Find out what happens in Part 2 of Vinnie Bang Bang & the Chemical Punk Monkey: Generation PB82.